PARRISH BLUE

VANESSA MACLAREN-WRAY

Cover design copyright © 2021 by Niki Lenhart
nikilen-designs.com

Published by Water Dragon Publishing
waterdragonpublishing.com

An imprint of Paper Angel Press
paperangelpress.com

ISBN 978-1-953469-81-6 (Trade Paperback)

FIRST EDITION

10 9 8 7 6 5 4 3 2

AUTHOR'S NOTE

In pre-internet days, I had a chance to visit the Minneapolis Institute of Art. There, a brilliant, massive, fantastic (in every sense) painting captured my imagination: *Dream Castle in the Sky* by Maxfield Parrish. I kept wandering back to study that image, trying to memorize its colors and imagery, the story it told.

In Parrish's heyday, he was thought of primarily as a great illustrator—books, advertisements, and hugely popular posters. I discovered his work in a serious art museum.

I wondered: How will people see art in the future? What does art have to tell us about the worlds we dream of?

Therefore, this story.

PARRISH BLUE

HE DIDN'T BELONG AT MAXFIELD'S. That lime-green solar jacket and striped sunhat screamed *tourist* in Southport, where no one strayed beyond the protective canopies. The stout, long-haired young man hurriedly peeled off the offending items, but the damage was already done. He'd made it through the crystal-glazed entry doors, but would never be welcomed further into this exclusive domain, reserved for the most-deserving of Earth's elite.

Sallie Anaro, emerging from the subtle hidden slider of the staff entrance, couldn't help but watch the familiar routine. Three steps from the door, the poor yokel had to cope with Georges Lennard's masterful *maître d'* skills. Never rude, always immovable, Lennard had evicted far more presentable intruders. From her position, she couldn't hear their words, but the exchange proceeded all too clearly—Lennard's elegant gesture to the door, the man's flustered brush at his thin moustache and hesitant presentation of an old-fashioned ident card. Lennard's eyes glittered as his comtacts scanned the card and linked to the reservation system. There followed that rarest of conclusions: Lennard's bow of welcome, his arm extended to summon the coat-check clerk for the guest's cartoonish outerwear.

Sallie recognized elements of a familiar drama. The off-planet visitor would have accepted an invitation to rendezvous at Maxfield's, to play his role in an elegant young creature's scheme. The escort (or rather, the escorted one) would arrive stylishly late, draw attention to themself, and generally exhibit themself—with the goal of attachment to a holder of railship stock. At Maxfield's, a suitably attractive fortune-seeker would be perceived as in need of rescue from inferior company, that liberation to be provided by one whose social status led them to dine regularly at this most elegant of retreats.

The inadequate partner, having served their purpose, would be discarded, often before the conclusion of the meal. The mark would be left with the bill, and waitstaff could expect no more than the minimum gratuity. At least such unfortunates were usually respectful to servers, if only to avoid further humiliation.

As Lennard lifted an eyebrow for her attention, Sallie looked away. She flicked her eyes to activate her comtacts and scanned the accessible-staff list, highlighting those associates who might come to *her* rescue. No one, not even her dear friend Enanci, so much as blinked a response to her urgent message.

She turned to scan the real-world space. In person, Enanci would be more vulnerable to persuasion.

Oh, well.

Leveraging her assets, Enanci leaned into her elaboration of the evening specials for the visual and auditory appreciation of a large table of elegantly-attired heirs and heiresses. She had no incentive to liberate Sallie from the role of supporting player in tonight's cruel social drama.

Acknowledging Lennard's summons, Sallie mustered a smile she hoped didn't betray too much, and approached the awkward customer. The gentle whisper of her Winsome Sylph costume as it swayed to her walk was enough to draw his attention.

"This way, sir." She led the unwitting soul to one of the better *tables aux deux*, one with an unobstructed view of the entry.

Lennard maintained his outer *sang-froid*, but used his executive override to eye-beam an irritated stream of scowling faces across her visual field. While the transmission line held, Sallie eye-beamed back a rapid series of increasingly cheerful faces. As she closed the link, she looked over her shoulder to Lennard with a cheery smile.

Lennard's face betrayed nothing, but she knew he'd be seething. *Let him sulk. The least I can do is give the poor dupe a good seat for his date's grand entrance— a once-in-a-lifetime opportunity.*

While Sallie hadn't invested in physical enhancements like Enanci's, she had developed a flair for making customers comfortable that earned her those essential rent-paying tips. With a barely-noticeable adjustment to local sound settings, a repositioning of tableware to fit the individual's reach, and a shift of the centerpiece to clear his view, she soon had her new customer noticeably relaxed and scanning the pricey menu with scarcely a bead of sweat on his brow.

When she swept by a few minutes later with a crystal goblet of nanite-purified and precision-mineralized water, he was at ease enough to decline her offer of a cocktail and request, of all things, "A glass of fruit juice, please."

Sallie closed her lips over the list of the day's special cocktails. Fruit juice? Was he unaware that Maxfield's offered a diverse array of mixed drinks? Many of the elite abhorred alcohol.

"If you have anything so mundane in that four-star kitchen," he added, grey eyes twinkling as the chandelier crystals shifted overhead. He lifted the empty wine glass and swirled an imaginary nectar. "You might have to ask the sommelier for *l'essence des pommes* or *le vin sans puissance*."

She imagined Gerard, his bulbous nose twitching over a glass of well-aged *pinot noir*, responding to such a request. "Oh, I daresay it will cost me my employment, good sir," Sallie replied. "But I will see what I can obtain while Chef is otherwise occupied."

A tall carafe of white grape juice, which she did in fact snag unobserved during a peak in kitchen activity, earned her a light, conspiratorial smile from him. Did this tourist already know the evening would be a charade for his date's benefit, not his? Could it be he was a willing partner in the game?

The evening bustle picked up, and Sallie needed to devote her attention to the high-and-mighty who claimed her premium tables. The mayor coasted in with a crew of capitalists pitching a new railship expansion project. The need for increased capacity made no sense to Sallie. Why would any sane person spend days cramped in a tin can to visit some stinking outpost planet ... let alone pack up their belongings and leave civilization forever?

By no coincidence, a table adjacent to the mayor's hosted a MicroFirm director celebrating a milestone by treating his top team to an evening's luxury. From the alcohol consumption—all at the expense of the company— Sallie anticipated she'd be flashing at least two urgent messages to Lennard to summon his white-glove removals crew. She also made a mental note to check the markets later and put in a quick buy order to supplement her portfolio. Meanwhile, there were the High Town baronets and their expensive spouses to be catered to. Not to mention their progeny, doomed to feast like royalty when what they hungered for would not be found in an uptown bistro.

In the meantime, her solo customer sipped his *vin sans puissance* and watched the entryway with an air of pleasurable anticipation. Eventually, she felt compelled to approach and suggest an appetizer.

"Something to tide you over until your guest arrives, sir," she offered. "There's no breach of etiquette."

"Oh," he said, one eyebrow wrinkling in puzzlement. "But I'm not waiting for anybody. I'm on my own. Gram's solicitor sent me down here. He said, 'You simply must see Maxfield's before you head home.' And he was right, so right." His eyes slid away from Sallie's and back to the entryway. The dreamy, contented stare reasserted itself.

"But ..." Sallie hesitated. "What ...?"

This time, when she followed the tourist's line of sight, she realized he wasn't looking at the entrance. He was gazing at the wall above the entry doors. The towering expanse stretched to the white band of illusory clerestory windows high overhead. As if one would ever allow sunlight to penetrate indoors.

The wall that held his attention supported the trademark image Sallie never even noticed anymore: the oversized light-painting that gave the restaurant its name. Diners enjoyed the illusion that they looked out from a fairy-tale castle over an imaginary landscape of rivers, rocks, more castles, and mountains beyond mountains. It made for a pleasant enough background, but she never understood what people saw in the high-tech display.

Mar-El Parelli's ten-by-sixteen-meter rendition of Maxfield Parrish's *Romance* glowed with an impossibly luminous, shimmering light made possible by MicroFirm's patented image-generation components. The recreation shone with the light of one and a half billion pixel-equivalents, rendered in self-renewing emissive biocels. Strictly speaking, Parelli's work was no more than a copy, but the artist considered it his masterwork. To the owners of Maxfield's, this version was the completed work—to them, the twentieth-century painting was nothing more than an early sketch.

The restaurant offered its patrons other Parrish reproductions: a series of hand-counterfeited canvases along the south wall, several culturally-updated Arabian Nights posters adorning the restrooms, the faux-mythic-Greek costuming for the waitstaff. However, Mr. First-Nighter's eager eyes fixed only on the massive Parelli. At least the server script did not require Sallie to respond with anything more complex than "May I take your order, then, sir?"

The order transmitted, she moved on to the next table. She remained puzzled as to why this plebeian soul would spend a fortune on high-society cuisine in order to look at a computerized version of an image as saccharine as its title.

The tourist gave away snippets of his tale over the course of the evening, stretching the meal out by ordering first an appetizer, then one of Chef Milland's multi-course *spécialités*, followed up with a Brazilian coffee.

While arranging his appetizer—a deep-fried carnation nestled in an arrangement of *crudités*—Sallie learned that he had come home from Cruzamiel to settle certain financial issues on his grandparents' estates. Though she said nothing, Sallie hoped the estate attorney had warned his client how much the evening's account might affect his remaining share of that settlement.

When the new busboy managed to knock over the fruit-juice carafe while hurrying with an overloaded tray, her customer laughed understandingly as he dodged the flood. He brushed aside Sallie's apologies and held the centerpiece as she slipped off the soaked tablecloth and swept a clean one into place.

"My Grandmas and Grandpa were among the original immigrants to Cruzamiel, if you can believe that," he said as she worked to reset the table. "The trip alone took nearly fifty years, hopscotching through found wormholes. By the time Dad came of age, they'd built the bridge network, so the old folks sent him home to Earth for college. Did you ever know anyone who used that system? The one before the barons built their so-called

Railway to the Stars? On the bridge tour, the trip from Cruz to Earth still took Dad over a year, both ways. What with taking an advanced degree and falling in love, he didn't get home for nearly eight years. Swore he'd never leave Cruzamiel again and kept the promise." His glance drifted back to that glowing wall.

As she listened, Sallie rearranged the place-setting for the second course and reviewed his order to be sure she hadn't forgotten any necessary silverware.

"Dad never understood why I wanted to travel," he rambled on. "Mom put money aside, bit by bit, but it was never enough. You know how it is. But then the barons got together and built the trans-stellar line and the railship idea took off and here we are, just a week's ride away from the furthest outer worlds."

He settled the centerpiece back in its place and looked to her for approval. She gave him a nod, just as she would have done for a fellow worker.

"When the family called for a volunteer to come sort out the old folks' business, I jumped at the chance. It's been fun. But Dad was right—there's no place like home. No offense, but except for that wall up there, there are no horizons like that here on Earth. Just imagine, once this planet had enough natural beauty that an artist could be inspired to see worlds that hadn't yet been discovered."

When she served bread (pan-flamed sourdough with feta), she was informed that Phoenix City on Cruzamiel was the second-to-last stop on the Great Western route. He described the bargain-priced ConRail journey as tedious, but bearable. For most of the trip, he'd shared a compartment with a family of well-fed tourists from

Gorovny, who talked through the entire journey to Nearly Home. For the last leg, his compartment-mate had been a solitary engineer who slept most of the way.

With soup (lemon leek with rosemary garnish), she learned his name was John Thomas Meriwether the Fourth, but that his family referred to him as Baby Johnny, while all his friends called him J.T. He guessed right the first time how Sallie spelled her name.

Over a spoonful of palate-cleansing sorbet (lime tinctured with cultured pomegranate), he smiled up at her, the glow of the bio-art wall in his eyes, and said, "Alejandro was right, it is just like home."

Distracted by the need to balance the empty soup bowl just so, Sallie replied, "The soup? The sorbet?"

That made him laugh out loud—a soft, musical laugh that nonetheless triggered sidelong glances and frowns from nearby tables.

"The view," he explained. He gestured behind her with a spoonful of golden crystals.

She turned and for the first time—she felt sure now it was the very first time—she *saw* Parrish/Parelli's painting. The mountains shimmered with an unearthly aura, evening light glowing on their shoulders. Above the stone towers clustered on the mountainside, a mystical silver light glistened in the hanging snowfields of higher mountains that rose peak upon peak into the far distance. The calm pool in the foreground, the still reflections glowing within, the dark columns binding earth and sky, and the human figures caught in a moment of stillness ... everything in the image beckoned to her from an alternate universe of light and balance.

Sallie wanted to reach out and tap the shoulder of that woman in the image, the one who had turned away from the view.

What are you thinking? she wanted to ask. *Who are you thinking about?*

The scene blurred as if a cloud had condensed in the air between her and the image. Sallie turned away, dipping her head as though to keep track of the trace of soup swirling at the bottom of the bowl. "Your entrée should be ready in a moment, sir."

Sallie had a few seconds to clear her eyes while waiting for Chef to plate J.T.'s entrée (braised brochette of hand-spliced lamb pod, in a light cream sauce with a touch of honey-crossed garlic). With the entrée delivered, she held her composure long enough to summon the sommelier for the mayor's final-course *accompagnement* and complete the processing of a baronet's charge-plate. For once, Sallie did not blink down to check on her gratuity; she had urgent business elsewhere.

Claiming the break she was due, Sallie slipped upstairs to the ladies' room on the mezzanine—the one set aside for private parties on that level. Along the way, she took one detour, to retrieve her makeup bag from the lockers behind the kitchen. That proved wise, because before she had completed a check that the restroom was truly empty, Sallie dissolved into tears.

I'm coming down with something. A new allergy. Asthma. Sensitivity to gene-spliced spices. Thinking abstractly helped to distract her, but those tears evolved to sobs, not sneezes. *I need to be back on the floor, and soon.* She snatched at facial wipes and tossed them into the disposer as quickly as they were used.

With no one else in the room, Sallie left off trying to fool herself. *How could that silly painting bring this on? I've seen it a thousand times.* In the half-decade she'd worked in its glow, that would be just about exactly how many times she'd ignored it.

Then again, how long had it been since she'd seen Earth's own sky unfiltered by protective canopies? Hadn't she dreamed once of mountains like that? *It's that tourist. He's thrown me off my game.*

She'd planned to soften the unhappy evening for a bumpkin manipulated by a social climber, by treating him like a regular. Instead, the man from Cruzamiel had treated Maxfield's like his own hometown café, with Sallie his regular server. Or a friend he knew who happened to work there. That wistful expression that flowed over his face when he looked up at the painting ... she wanted to know if she'd had that expression tonight, when she'd looked at it with him.

Even unexpected tears can't go on forever. Soon enough, Sallie's dispassionate side could take over. After a quick splash of water to clear the worst of the damage, she leaned in close to the mirror.

The same face had stared back at her over her own bathroom sink this morning, but now she saw something else in those eyes, a sense of fear and promise. She remembered that feeling from the day she'd signed over half her income in the lease papers for her precious, tiny apartment. That was how she'd proven to herself she hadn't run away from home again; she was truly independent. She'd make her own way, forget her childhood fantasies, and overcome her mother's challenge: *I couldn't make it; neither will you.*

Five years later, she could still hear herself shrilling into her mother's reddened face, "I'm going! I can't stand this block of concrete nothingness anymore! I want to live somewhere beautiful! Everything here is ugly, ugly, ugly—especially you!" What she couldn't remember was what her mother said to that, because Sallie had been slapping the faulty latch panel with every screech of "ugly." When the door finally responded, she plunged through without a backward glance.

Now, Sallie looked into the watery, bloodshot eyes of the woman in the mirror and murmured, so that the sound whispered like a distant waterfall in a golden canyon, "I want to live somewhere beautiful."

Southport was certainly Somewhere. All the beautiful people came here to be seen. Oceans of lovely money washed over the shores of the local economy, much of it settling at Maxfield's. Southport trumpeted its art museums, public sculptures, cultural events, concerts, and theatrical performances—all the most beautiful sights and sounds of the civilized world.

Every day, Sallie stepped into the most chic, adorable, artistic bistro in the city's exclusive High Town district. She knew the rich, the pampered, and the powerful by name and by favorite libation. Every evening, when she changed out of her sylphish uniform and strolled out onto the mall, she knew that heads turned to follow her. Sallie sometimes envied the embraceable beauty of her friend Enanci, but she had learned to be satisfied with her own style, mirroring the ice-crystal fashion of the High Town elite.

Sallie shook the cobwebs out of her head, blew her nose, and checked the mirror again. A few eye drops flushed away the redness as well as the last of the tears. A moment with her makeup kit, and no one would ever know. She washed her hands once more, letting the music of running water fill her ears. The sound seemed to flow outwards, beyond Maxfield's, into the elegant streets of High Town, through the shaded, sterile colonnades of Southport.

I want to live somewhere beautiful.

Every day, I want light to fill my eyes.

Barely five minutes later, restored to surface normality, Sallie brought J.T. his coffee (whole-grown vanilla walnut, double-caffeinated, fresh-ground, and brewed on demand). He didn't ask why the cup rattled when she set it on the saucer. He had no way to know her hands were never that unsteady.

J.T. hesitated at the dessert menu, but Sallie, maintaining the role of solicitous server, persuaded him that a simple mousse would be the perfect finish.

When it became clear that he would linger beyond final seating, as the new aristocrats began to lead their entourages off to the next engagement, Sallie became an off-duty server with the power of making dessert in a lonely restaurant more than acceptable.

She brewed two fresh coffees, asked Chef to plate a second mousse, and took for herself the unclaimed chair at J.T.'s table.

He studied her face in quick glances, a smile quirking the corners of his mouth. She knew her eyes would look strange, as they flickered through the colorful messages from her manager, concerning tomorrow's schedule, and those from a fellow waitstaff member, who wondered if her friend would ever go home. A little talk of the mountains of

Cruzamiel made for a fine conclusion to the evening, and by then Sallie's eyes glimmered only with reflections of the painting on the wall.

■　　■　　■

Just over four months later, Enanci watched Sallie pack, promised to write, agreed to adopt the ratcat, and protested the whole while.

"It's been hardly any time since you met this off-world yahoo. What are you thinking? I know what you've saved. It's barely enough for a one-way ticket! Do you have any idea how long it will take you to save up for a return? It's nothing like civilized out there."

Good-byes took no time at all, thanks to rigorous security at the spaceport. As she settled her bags into the compartment, Sallie caught a fingernail on the edge of the lease-release doc. She tried to think about the hard-won apartment, her sliver of city view, and could barely even remember why she had tied herself to such a place. She pushed the sharp-edged doc firmly to the back of her case and turned to greet her traveling companions. They were a family of five, on their way to Kittaning, with a tortoiseshell cat hidden in a soft-sided bag.

Between playing with the cat (with a twinge of regret for her own cuddly ratcat) and listening to the middle child talk non-stop, Sallie had little time for second-guessing her decision. The journey to Kittaning would take a night and two full days, but they found plenty to pass the time in the steerage-grade compartment. When games grew tedious or the children needed to sleep, the adults took turns scrolling through the various flight perspectives on the viewport screen.

Early in the morning of the second day, the cat and Sallie enjoyed a solitary hour as the family redeemed coupons for observation-level seating. Neither left-out traveler wasted any time on envy. Sallie had a credit for an hour's entertainment—a gift from Enanci for just such an occasion—but instead she left her comtacts in their case and stretched out across the seats for a nap. The cat spent a blissful hour curled up behind Sallie's knees.

After a brief layover in Kittaning, and the sadness of parting from new friends, the compartment felt lonely, not private. Sallie paged impatiently through the stale, second-hand sights on the viewport. She thought she'd wash up, get ready for the next day, but the lighting in the tiny water-closet made her skin look pale and grey.

Am I ill? Enanci's parting speech rang in her ears: "You are *sick*, gal-o-mino. You've got sun-madness." *Was she right? Am I crazy?*

From Gorovny to Cruzamiel would take only seven hours, instead of the years-long hopscotch endured by the original immigrants.

Some of them are still alive, Sallie remembered. *Will I meet them?*

She'd repacked her bags and stacked them by the door long before the bells pealed and the announcement came through for her section to disembark. The exit route led through a maze of corridors and mysterious doorways. Passengers were supposed to follow directions scrolling across their comtacts, but Sallie allowed the flow of the crowd to carry her on and out to the sweet clean air.

At last, the indignities of security scans and visa checks and queries about the contents of baggage came to an end. She stood in the midst of a milling mass of commuters, tourists, and other immigrants. Like her, the other newcomers peered at the directional signs and wondered what to do next. The general consensus among the immigrants seemed to sum up to: find transport to downtown, locate short-term lodgings, and tap into the job listings.

Suddenly, J.T. appeared at her side, nervously smoothing his uncooperative mustache and pushing his hair out of his face. "Would you like some help with all this?"

Yes, of course she would.

What she really wanted was to fling her arms around him, but she wasn't sure whether she'd burst into tears or laughter. Either way, there were too many people around. She had time now—she could save that moment for later.

Snagging the tethers of both her suitcases and giving a firm tug to get them floating straight, J.T. led her to a travel-all that hardly looked big enough to transport two people, let alone Sallie's luggage.

"It's not mine yet, you understand," he admitted. "But I got it down to a five-year loan."

Together, they managed to wrangle the bags into the van's unforgiving cargo space.

"Sorry," she apologized. "It didn't look like so much when I was cleaning out my apartment." When she was packing, every item she chose seemed special and irreplaceable. Now, she'd have left half her bags behind if it could erase the look on his face that said, *I should have signed for a bigger loan.*

"It's all right," he said, as they teamed up to push the rear hatch closed. "See? Everything fits just perfectly." He slipped his arm over her shoulders, and she slid her arm around his waist, and yes, he was right. Everything was perfect.

Sallie pressed her face to the window for one last look at the station as they pulled away. Those other new arrivals gaping at the glowing sky and distant peaks became tourists.

Unlike them, she'd arrived home.

■　　　■　　　■

Years later, Sallie happened across her old filecase in the back of a storage bin and lingered over it for hours. She found the letters of reference she'd carried that day from Georges Lennard, Chef Milland, and even Southport's mayor, bundled with the old doc containing her lease-release.

"Yes, of course I remember Maxfield's," J.T. said that night, as they stood together enjoying the canyon view and pretending there were no rowdy grandchildren barely asleep in the cottage behind them.

Summer sunlight poured like molten gold along the upper ridges, casting an evanescent glow on the mist gathering along the river below. She took J.T.'s hand as a clutter of old images swept through her mind: the chaos of Chef's territory, the hauteur of the customers, the art in the background. She'd toiled for so many years alongside those ancient views of Cruzamiel and never imagined it could possibly be real—glimmering meadows, iridescent forests, and castles in the sky.

"Wait, now, it's coming."

They left off reminiscence to catch the summer twilight sweeping over the sky, leaping from rocky peak to rocky peak with the liquid joy of Parrish blue.

ABOUT THE AUTHOR

Vanessa MacLaren-Wray is an award-winning author and poet who also builds robots, creates photographs, and works towards a more climate-safe world. She grew up in a military family, which meant constant moves: adapting to new worlds, new ways of speaking, and new cultures. Her first book, *All That Was Asked*, is a first-contact science fiction tale. No, of course it isn't based on her childhood. Or is it?

She does not claim to be able to prepare any of the dishes offered at Maxfield's. However, she has received compliments on her homemade jams and owns the secret to her grandmother's pumpkin pie.

To learn more about Vanessa and her world and her work, visit her at *Cometary Tales* (*cometarytales.com*).

ALSO BY THE AUTHOR

ALL THAT WAS ASKED

by Vanessa MacLaren-Wray

It was supposed to be an easy jaunt to observe the stick-like aliens of Deep Valley Universe.

SHADOWS OF INSURRECTION

BOOK ONE OF THE UNREMEMBERED KING

by Vanessa MacLaren-Wray

Once in a generation, the matriarchs of Jeska choose a new king.

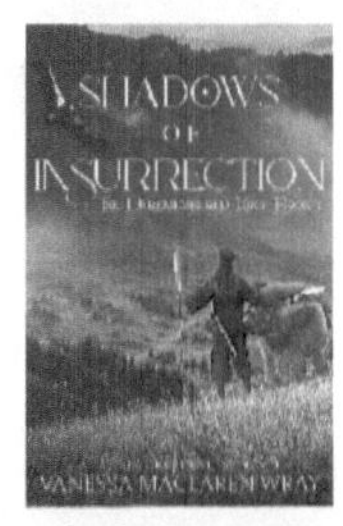

FLAMES OF ATTRITION

BOOK TWO OF THE UNREMEMBERED KING

by Vanessa MacLaren-Wray

The nation of Jeska stands at a crossroads.

THE SMUGGLERS

FROM THE TRUCK STOP AT THE CENTER OF THE GALAXY

by Vanessa MacLaren-Wray

Mother says, "Don't name the merchandise," and "Don't let the humans see you."

YOU MIGHT ALSO ENJOY

BEST SERVED COLD
by Bob Schoonover

A dish of corporate greed served with a side of revenge.

HOT DROP
by J Dark

What starts as a rescue mission in a combat zone on a hostile planet becomes something more.

REDUCTION IN FORCE
by Steve Soult

A revolutionary memory erasure procedure may be Gil Schaffer's only hope for salvation, but the price could be greater than he bargained for.

Available in digital and trade paperback editions from
Water Dragon Publishing
waterdragonpublishing.com